D0562405

THE
SQUIRRELS
HAVE GONE
NUTS

ALSO BY JOE McGEE

Junior Monster Scouts series

The Monster Squad

Crash! Bang! Boo!

It's Raining Bats and Frogs!

Monster of Disguise

Trash Heap of Terror

Curse of the Crummy Mummy!

Night Frights series

The Haunted Mustache

The Lurking Lima Bean

The Not-So-Itsy-Bitsy Spider

NIGHT FRIGHTS

#4

THE SQUIRRELS HAVE GONE NUTS

BY **JOE McGEE**

ILLUSTRATED BY **TEO SKAFFA**

ALADDIN

New York London Toronto
Sydney New Delhi

ALADDIN

An imprint of Simon & Schuster Children's Publishing Division
1230 Avenue of the Americas, New York, New York 10020
First Aladdin paperback edition September 2022
Text copyright © 2022 by Joseph McGee
Illustrations copyright © 2022 by Teo Skaffa
Also available in an Aladdin hardcover edition.
All rights reserved, including the right of reproduction in whole or in part in any form.
ALADDIN and related logo are registered trademarks of Simon & Schuster, Inc.
For information about special discounts for bulk purchases, please contact Simon & Schuster Special Sales at 1-866-506-1949 or business@simonandschuster.com.
The Simon & Schuster Speakers Bureau can bring authors to your live event. For more information or to book an event contact the Simon & Schuster Speakers Bureau at 1-866-248-3049 or visit our website at www.simonspeakers.com.
Designed by Tiara Iandiorio
The text of this book was set in Adobe Garamond Pro.
Manufactured in the United States of America 0722 OFF
10 9 8 7 6 5 4 3 2 1
Library of Congress Control Number 2022933718
ISBN 9781534480988 (hc)
ISBN 9781534480971 (pbk)
ISBN 9781534480995 (ebook)

To Shane, Zachary, Logan, Ainsley, Sawyer, and Braeden—the Trap Pond Crew . . . and also to the squirrel I hit with that football

THE
SQUIRRELS
HAVE GONE
NUTS

Greetings, friends . . . once again, it is I, the Keeper, your mysterious guide into the strange and unexplainable events of Wolver Hollow. By now, you may have experienced some, or all, of the other thrilling and chilling tales of weirdness that have befallen this quirky little town. Or perhaps you are new to these dark shadows and even darker secrets. But whether you have been here before, or are visiting for the first time, I must warn you—what I am about to share with you is a tale so terrifying, so shocking, that even I have trouble believing that it ever happened. But happen it did, and so, without further ado, let me take you to that fateful, sweltering summer, and a boy by the name of Dillon . . . Dillon Ford.

1

"Dillon!"

Thump . . . Thump . . . Thump . . .

"Dillon Ford!" called his mom, from the
bottom of the stairs.

Thump . . . Thump . . . Thump . . .

"I know you can hear me! Stop bounc-
ing that tennis ball against your wall and go
outside!"

Dillon lay on his bed, head at the foot of

it and feet planted on the wall. One foot on either side of his Captain Duke Ross, Galactic Hero poster. Duke Ross pointed one gloved finger at Dillon and stared right at him. I WANT YOU FOR THE MARS EXPEDITIONARY FORCE read the caption at the bottom of the poster.

Dillon tossed the tennis ball against the wall again—*thump*—and caught it.

"But it's so hot outside," he hollered back.

"Do *not* make me come up there!" Mom said.

"But there's nothing to do!"

Thump.

"Find something to do!"

"I am!"

Thump.

"Something besides driving me crazy with that tennis ball!" Mom said.

Dillon groaned and threw the ball against the wall one last time.

Thump.

"Fine," he said. "I'll go outside."

"Thank you," said Mom.

"But if I die of heatstroke, it won't be my fault," Dillon said.

"I'll send you out with plenty of lemonade," said Mom. "Crisis averted."

Dillon swung his legs off the bed, pulled on his sneakers, and shuffled out of his bedroom. Maybe Mikey was home, he thought. Mikey Dillman was his best friend and lived next door. The Dillmans had gone on a family camping trip, and Dillon had been bored out of his mind all week. If the station wagon was in the driveway, that would mean they were finally home. Dillon's tree house had a perfect view over the hedge wall that separated his house from Mikey's.

As promised, Mom had a full water bottle of lemonade waiting for him.

"Thank you," said Dillon, taking a big swig. He tossed the tennis ball up and caught it. "I'll be in my base, drinking my own sweat when the lemonade runs out."

"Oh, knock it off," Mom said. "Before you know it, summer will be over and you'll be back in school. You'll wish you had these long, lazy, hot days of summer vacation."

Dillon shrugged and, with tennis ball in hand, headed out the back door.

 7

The tree house had been built into the thick limbs and full canopy of a mighty oak tree, right at the edge of their property. It had two floors, a small balcony, and windows with shutters you could close for secret meetings. A ladder had been built into the trunk for access (the tree house was at least ten feet high), and one long limb stretched over the hedges and into Mikey's yard. His parents had agreed not to cut it down and, instead, had made a rope ladder so that Mikey could get up there from his own yard.

Dillon and Mikey referred to the tree house as their "base" and decided that they were members of Captain Duke Ross's Mars Expeditionary Force. After all, the poster did say that Captain Ross wanted *them* for the force. They usually sat up there reading *Galactic Hero* comics, drinking soda, and playing board games.

But when Dillon climbed up the ladder and into the base and peered out over the hedges, he did not see the Dillmans' RV, just their station wagon sitting in the drive-way. That, and Mikey's older brother Mark's beat-up pizza delivery car with the PIZZA MARIO sign still stuck to the top of it.

He picked up the stack of comics and dropped them back down on the table. He'd already reread them a dozen times, and the new issue wouldn't come out for another couple of weeks. Playing board games by yourself was no fun. He thought about going

 9

down to the creek, or maybe the park, but that meant walking (or skateboarding), and it was entirely too hot to do either.

Then he saw it.

A big gray squirrel with an even bigger bushy tail and a white patch of fur on its chin. It had something in its mouth. Something shiny. Something that looked awfully familiar. *It can't be,* Dillon thought.

Dillon spun around and pulled open the base's candy basket. All the Sour Sugar Snakes packages were empty. Every. Single. One. And the culprit was clinging to the side of a tree, with a package in its mouth!

"Hey!" Dillon shouted, rushing back out to the small balcony. "Hey, that's my Sour Sugar Snakes, you thief! Get back here!"

The squirrel shook its tail and scampered up the side of the other tree.

"Give it back!"

Dillon threw the tennis ball as hard as he could.

He wanted to hit the tree. He wanted to scare the squirrel enough that it would drop his last pack of Sour Sugar Snakes and run away.

 11

But he did not hit the tree.

He hit the squirrel. Directly. It fell backward, away from the tree, and landed on its back, in Dillon's yard.

"Squirrel?" Dillon called. "Are you okay?"

The squirrel did not answer. It lay very, very still, its tail sticking straight out and the package of Sour Sugar Snakes in its mouth.

2

Dillon stood over the squirrel. It definitely wasn't moving. Maybe it was stunned, he thought. Yeah, that was it. It was just taking a nap, sleeping it off. He thought about nudging it with his foot, but then he thought about it waking up and biting him on the toe. He liked his toes and did not like the thought of a squirrel biting one. Squirrel teeth are sharp! In the end, he opted for a stick.

"Squirrel?" he asked.

He gently poked the squirrel with the stick.

Nothing.

"Mr. Squirrel, are you okay?"

He poked it again. This time just a little bit harder.

Still nothing.

"It was only a tennis ball," Dillon said. "I wasn't even trying to hit you."

Dillon poked the squirrel a third time. One could never be *too* sure. The foil-wrapped bag of Sour Sugar Snakes fell out of the squirrel's mouth. Dillon used the stick to pull the candy closer to him and then snatched it up. There was still a chance that the squirrel would come to and scamper after him, and he wasn't going to have any digits near it when that happened. He shoved the candy into his pocket.

But after five minutes, it became very evident that that was not going to happen.

Dillon felt horrible.

"Squirrels are supposed to be quick, right?" he said. "And I have the worst aim ever. Like that time at the Wolver Hollow carnival when Sheriff Macklin was in the dunk tank and I wanted to dunk him so bad. And then I threw the ball and missed the entire target by, like, a mile and hit old Ms. Applewhite, who was carrying her prized apple-berry pie. She dropped the tray, right on Madeline Harper's dog, Tucker, who bolted into the middle of Mayor Stine's domino re-creation of the town, knocking it all over right before he placed the last domino. Mayor Stine was so angry he threw his hat in the air . . . which hit a floating balloon that drifted into the power line and shorted the electricity, shutting down all the rides."

The squirrel just lay there.

"So, my point is," said Dillon, "that I wasn't supposed to actually hit you."

He still didn't feel any better. He couldn't just leave the squirrel here, in his backyard, directly at the bottom of his base. He owed the squirrel a proper burial at least.

"I'll be right back."

Dillon crossed the yard and went back into the house. He knew exactly what he could use to put the squirrel in.

"Dillon Ford, you are not coming in yet,"

Mom said. "You haven't even been out there for half an hour."

"I just need to get something from my room," he said.

"Make it quick."

Dillon had a pretty big collection of Duke Ross trading cards. He and Mikey had been collecting and trading for years. He kept his cards in a shoebox under his bed. Summer would be over soon, and the school year was right around the corner. That meant school shopping. That meant new sneakers, and new sneakers meant a new shoebox. So he could use his card collection box now and replace it when he got his new kicks.

He took the cards out of the box and was about to leave his room when he had another

17

idea. He grabbed a marker from his desk and wrote as neatly as he could across the lid of the shoebox: *MR. SQUIRREL, RIP.*

Then he added: *Hit by a tennis ball . . . by accident.*

Then he scribbled under that: *Caught stealing Sour Sugar Snakes.*

And finally he added: *But still, it was an accident. Sorry.*

He added his initials for good measure: *DF.*

He lined the bottom of the box with two mismatched socks (the matching sock partners had been missing for a month now), pushed the lid on, and carried it out into the backyard. But when he got to the place where the squirrel had been, should be, it wasn't there. No squirrel. Nothing.

Mr. Squirrel.
RIP
Hit by a tennis ball...
by accident.
Caught stealing
Sour Sugar Snakes.
But still, it was an
accident.
Sorry.
DF

McGeezy

McGeezy

"Squirrel?" Dillon asked. He looked around the yard. It must have been okay, he thought. It must have sprung up and climbed into one of the trees.

Then something bounced off the top of his head.

"Ouch!" he said.

Then another. Then three more.

 19

Plunk. Plunk. Plunk. Plunk.

All on the top of his head.

"What the heck?"

Acorns. Four acorns lay scattered around his feet. Dillon slowly raised his head. There was his squirrel. The one with the white patch on its chin. The one he'd knocked out of the tree. But he wasn't alone. The entire branch was filled with squirrels. Angry-looking squirrels, all armed with paws full of acorns.

Plunk. Plunk. Plunk. Plunk. Plunk. Plunk.

Acorns rained down on Dillon.

"Ow, quit it! That's enough! Hey, watch it!"

He covered his head and ran for the house, but the entire roof was packed with squirrels. Instead, he dashed the other way, toward his base. He dropped the shoebox and climbed the ladder as fast as he could. As soon as he reached the tree house, he slammed the door shut and closed the window shutters.

There was no doubt about it—he was under siege.

3

"Dillon? Dillon, I'm going to the store!"

Dillon peeked out through the shutters.
Mom was standing on the back step, purse
over her shoulder. More squirrels had joined
the squirrel army on the roof. Easily over a
hundred of them, standing shoulder to shoulder, some staring at the tree house and some
peering down at Mom.

"Dillon, did you hear me?" she said. "I said

22

I'm going to the store to get something for dinner. Do you want anything?"

"I want the squirrels to go away?" he said.

"Me too," said Mom. "They're always getting into the bird feeders. Okay, be back shortly."

The back door banged shut behind her and a minute later, the sound of the old station wagon engine roared to life in the driveway. Dillon ran to the other window and peered out. Mom's car backed out of the driveway, muffler rattling, and out onto the street. A dozen squirrels clung to the top of her station wagon as she rumbled down the street, toward the market.

Mom's in danger, he thought. Why else would the squirrels be on her car? *Twelve* of

 23

them? They were clearly out for revenge.

"Not if I can help it," Dillon said.

He couldn't leave the base, not yet. Not with the squirrels watching his every move. But he had to get a message out. Maybe Mikey would be home soon. Or maybe he could somehow reach his classmate Gilbert Blardle. Gilbert lived a few houses down, across the street.

Dillon grabbed a marker and a pizza-grease-stained napkin from last weekend when he and Mikey had had a pizza party sleepover in the tree house and wrote a note. It read:

Help! Trapped in tree house. Surrounded by angry squirrels. —Dillon Ford

Dillon opened the trunk in the corner of the tree house. It was filled with all kinds of things: a telescope, an old pirate hat, a kite, some board games, his book report that he was supposed to turn in before summer break (so that's where it went! He'd been looking all over for that), and there it was—his battery-operated, remote-control air glider.

The Styrofoam body was nice and light, and the long plastic wingspan let it glide along with the power of the battery-operated propeller. Dillon checked both the plane and the remote. Green lights indicated that everything was charged and ready to go. He attached his napkin note to the wheel strut with a rubber band and opened one of the shutters.

"Here goes nothing," he said.

He threw the air glider out the tree house's window as if he were throwing a dart. It glided out over his backyard, and then Dillon pushed forward on the remote's power stick. The plastic propeller whined to life, and the air glider climbed up into the air.

Dillon pushed the left joystick, tilting the

 26

wing flaps so the glider would arc toward Gilbert's house. Gilbert was usually out in his yard playing soccer (fútbol, as he insisted on calling it), and if Dillon could land (or crash, even) the air glider into his yard, Gilbert would find the note.

The air glider angled toward Mikey's yard, just high enough to clear the Dillmans' roof. But first it had to clear the power line that ran from the street pole to the Dillmans' house. Dillon gave it a little more power and pointed the nose up. He'd clear the line and glide over the rooftop, and then it was a straight shot to Gilbert's yard.

The squirrels had other plans.

"No, no, no, no!" said Dillon, pushing the power stick on his remote control. But it

 27

was already all the way up. The glider could not go any faster. Two squirrels scurried along the power line, heading right for the air glider. As soon as the glider neared them, they grabbed the wings with their little paws and tore them from the Styrofoam body. The wingless plane plummeted to the ground, crashing right into Mikey Dillman's backyard. And with it, his note.

Dillon threw the remote to the floor.

"There goes that plan," he said.

Then he heard it. The distinct sound of old Italian opera music. The Dillmans were home! Mr. Dillman was very fond of old Italian opera music, and whenever his family went camping in their old RV, Mr.

Dillman made sure to have an Italian opera mixtape ready.

Sure enough, the RV pulled into their driveway and stopped, with one final exhaust-pipe boom and bellow of black smoke. The doors opened and the Dillmans clambered out: Mrs. Dillman in her bright red felt hat, Mr. Dillman in his traditional suspenders and stained T-shirt, Mark Dillman with his headphones and PocketMusicPlayer (they were super popular, and Dillon wanted one so bad), and then finally, Mikey. He was holding one of those giant foam hands that you get at sporting events—the kind with the index finger pointing up—and WOLFPACK #1 was printed on it. The Dillmans must have gone to a ball game or something while they were on their trip.

Dillon grabbed another tennis ball from the bucket in the corner of the tree house. It was full of them. Then he leaned out, took aim, and chucked the ball at the Dillmans' metal trash cans.

It hit with a loud *CLANG*, but only Mikey heard it. Mark had his headphones on, Mr. Dillman was rummaging through the cab of the RV for something, and Mrs. Dillman had gone down to the mailbox.

"Psst, Mikey!" Dillon said.

Mikey looked up toward the tree house.

"Hey, Dillon!" Mikey said.

"Code red!" Dillon said. "I repeat, code red!"

Several acorns pelted the side of the tree

house, and Dillon heard a barrage of thumps and scurrying on the roof.

"Roger," Mikey said. "On my way!"

"Hurry!" Dillon yanked the shutter closed and waited for reinforcements. The war had begun.

 31

4

The moment Mikey knocked on the door
of the tree house, Dillon pulled it open. Mikey
scrambled inside—leaves in his hair, his shirt
torn, and a small scratch on his face.

"Are you okay?" Dillon asked.

Mikey collapsed onto one of the beanbags
and exhaled loudly.

"Yeah, but that was a close one. The
squirrels—"

"Have gone nuts!" Dillon finished.

"What in the name of Plutonian picklefish is going on?" Mikey asked.

Dillon rubbed his chin. "Well, I kinda, maybe, I mean I didn't mean to, but . . ." and he went on to tell Mikey what had happened with the squirrel this morning and the events leading up to the current situation.

"Your mom's in danger," Mikey said. "If they're on her car, they're after her."

"The whole town is in danger!" said Dillon. "Look at what happened to you. You barely escaped with your life!"

Mikey had told Dillon about how he had used the rope ladder to climb up onto the branch while squirrels chattered at him and threw acorns and sticks. Then some of them

 33

had chased him along the branch, grabbing his shirt and tearing it. He had been in such a hurry that he'd scratched his face on some twigs.

"They mean business," said Mikey.

"Well, so do I," said Dillon. "It was an accident. I said I was sorry. If those squirrels don't want to accept my apology, fine. But I'm not going to sit around and let them terrorize us, Mom, or our town. We need a plan."

"We need reinforcements," said Mikey. He held up his foam finger and said, "Hey, I have an idea. Let's get Madeline Harper. She's supersmart and knows how to strategize. No one can beat her at chess, so maybe she can help us figure this out."

"Good idea," said Dillon. "And maybe Samantha von Oppelstein. She's always

 35

talking about weird stuff, and this is definitely weird stuff."

"We're going to need a distraction, though," said Mikey.

Dillon cracked the shutter and scanned the yard. Squirrels sat on the trash cans and lined the fence. They raced along the power line. They sat at the edge of the roof, along the gutter, and perched atop the clothesline. They were everywhere, and they were all staring toward the tree house with their angry, beady little eyes.

Then something caught his attention. Not something . . . someone. Someone whistling his way down the sidewalk with a small black book in his hands and a bunch of pamphlets. Dillon had seen him before, outside the market, handing out those booklets about "the Way."

"Mikey, look," Dillon whispered.

Mikey joined Dillon at the shutter, and they both watched the whistling, smiling man stop and tuck one of those booklets into the Dillmans' mailbox. Then he was on his way to Dillon's house, completely unaware of the army of squirrels, who seemed none too pleased with his whistling. They turned their attention from the tree house to the whistling, pamphlet-distributing man.

"That's our distraction," said Mikey. "Quick, while they're not looking!"

Dillon grabbed a couple of tennis balls from the basket and shoved them into his pockets.

Mikey raised an eyebrow.

"What?" Dillon asked.

"Do you really think that's a good idea?" Mikey asked. "Isn't that what started this whole thing in the first place?"

"Just in case," said Dillon.

They threw open the hatch and climbed down the ladder.

There was a sudden commotion from the front yard. A lot of squeaking and chattering and someone yelling, "Hey! Hey, knock it off! That's—that's my book! Those are my pamphlets! Don't tear my pamphlets! Come back with my hair! Get back! Get back, all of you!"

Dillon and Mikey crept to the side of the house and peered around the corner. The man who had been handing out pamphlets was running for his life, down the street, pursued by two dozen squirrels. Another bunch of squirrels were tearing up his pamphlets, while one squirrel raced up the telephone pole with the man's fake head of hair.

It was a terrifying sight to behold.

"Come on," Dillon said. "Now's our chance."

"Roger that," Mikey said.

He and Mikey dashed to some nearby shrubs and

crouched low, waiting. They were sure that at any second, a horde of angry squirrels was going to rush in, leaping, and tearing, and biting, and scratching. But that didn't happen. The squirrels were still squeaking and chittering and shredding up the man's pamphlets. The squirrels in the trees turned their attention on the tree house, and two other groups of squirrels ran off in different directions: one group went north, running along the power lines and roofs, while the other group went in the direction of Wolf Creek, scurrying along the tops of fences and hopping through yards.

"Where do you think they're off to?" Mikey asked.

"I don't know," said Dillon, "but we'd bet-

ter hurry. I think they're up to something."

Mikey and Dillon took one last look to make sure they were in the clear, and then they kept low and dashed across the street, keeping behind the cover of cars and trees and houses and buildings as best they could.

5

Madeline Harper lived right down at the end of the street. She was in her backyard, throwing a Frisbee with her dog, Tucker, when Dillon and Mikey got there. Tucker was barking and growling at something in the trees.

"Tucker, *enough*," Madeline said. "What's gotten into you?"

When she saw the boys, she waved. They were all in the same fifth-grade class (there was only one fifth-grade class) at Wolver Hollow Elementary School.

"Hey, guys!" said Madeline. "Whatcha up to? Hey, cool foam finger!"

Normally, Tucker would run to the boys, tail wagging. He loved kids. But right now he was too busy barking at something in the trees. Too busy to stop for nice pets and scratches behind the ear.

"Thanks!" said Mikey. He held the foam hand up, index finger pointing toward the trees. "What's up with Tucker?"

"I don't know," said Madeline, "but he won't stop barking, and I can't get him to go inside. There's something up there, but I can't see what it is."

"Squirrels," said Dillon.

"What?" Madeline asked. "Squirrels? Can't be. He never goes crazy like this over squirrels. I mean, he'd chase them, but he doesn't bark his head off at them."

"These aren't normal squirrels," said Dillon. "They've gone nuts. They've formed an army, and they're terrorizing the town."

"Because Dillon nailed one with a tennis ball," Mikey added, poking Dillon's shoulder with the foam finger.

"Dude, cut it out," said Dillon. "I told you it was an accident!"

Madeline stared at Mikey and Dillon for a moment. Tucker continued to bark and growl.

"You're serious, aren't you?" she said.

Dillon nodded.

Above them, the branches shook and

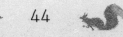

the leaves rustled. A pack of
beady-eyed squirrels appeared, cheeks
and paws packed with acorns. Their furry tails
twitched left and right, and the squirrels began
spitting acorns at them with deadly accuracy.

Tucker yelped as an acorn struck his
rear end.

"Ow!" Mikey yelled. An acorn struck
his arm so hard it felt as if it had been
fired from a slingshot.

A red welt was already forming. He covered his head with his foam hand.

Madeline quickly held her Frisbee over her head as more acorns flew down from above.

An acorn struck Dillon's shoulder and another hit Tucker, who turned tail and ran for the house.

"Run!" Dillon yelled. He grabbed Mikey and Madeline by the arm and pulled them away from the trees and the backyard.

"We can hide in my house," said Madeline.

"No time," said Dillon. "Besides, your family would be in danger."

"What are you talking about?" she asked, as they ran down the street.

"The squirrels are after me," said Dillon. "They're angry. And now they want their

46

revenge on me, even if that means terrorizing the town."

"What does terrorizing the town have to do with you?" Madeline asked.

"I don't know," said Dillon. "They're squirrels! Who said anything they do makes sense!"

"We figured that if anyone could come up with a plan, it would be you," Mikey said.

"Tell me everything," Madeline said.

By the time they'd reached the corner of Hill Crest and First Street, Dillon had filled Madeline in on everything that had happened.

When Dillon, Mikey, and Madeline reached Samantha von Oppelstein's house, they found her on her front step, broom in hand, facing half a dozen squirrels.

 47

"Shoo!" she said, swatting at two squirrels that darted toward her. "Go on! Get out of here!"

Across the street, a handful of squirrels ripped and tore at Ms. Thorn's prized rose-bushes. A pack of squirrels chased old Mr. MacNish up the sidewalk. He dropped his grocery bag and ran for his front door. Squirrels ran across rooftops and power lines and leapt onto the tops of cars. They knocked over garden gnome statues and toppled birdbaths.

The squirrels were on a rampage.

Samantha von Oppelstein swept three more squirrels off her step, one desperately clinging to the end of the broom.

"Samantha, duck!" Dillon yelled.

Samantha von Oppelstein hunched down as a squirrel leapt at her, claws out, just miss-

ing her hair. It hit the side of her house and
fell down, dazed.

"You guys!" she said. "*What* is going on?"

"Isn't it obvious?" asked Mikey. "Wolver
Hollow is under attack."

49

"By squirrels?" asked Samantha von Oppelstein.

"Never underestimate the power of an angry squirrel," said Dillon.

"We need to do something before it's too late," said Madeline.

A very loud crack interrupted them, followed seconds later by a thunderous boom.

"It may already be too late," said Dillon.

6

The loud crack and thunderous boom
sounded like they had come from the direction of the old windmill and the road that led north, out of town. The kids were halfway there, running as fast as they could, eyes peeled for any sign of a squirrel ambush, when another crack and another boom sounded.

There was no doubt about it: whatever was going on was going on just outside of town.

Dillon, Mikey, Madeline, and Samantha von Oppelstein cut behind the Wild Hunt restaurant and poured out onto North Main Street.

"They blocked the road!" Mikey said. He pointed his foam finger at the obstacle.

Two huge trees lay across the road, completely blocking it from any possible vehicle passage.

"They're trying to trap us in town," Madeline said. "It's like chess. They're setting up a box in order to corner us."

"So how do we *not* get cornered?" Dillon asked.

"The thing about traps," said Madeline, "is that you have to be tactically alert at all times. Otherwise, your opponent slips out from your setup and then you have to react to their surprise move."

"So what's our surprise move?" asked Mikey.

"Don't know yet," said Madeline.

Samantha von Oppelstein stepped forward, her broom resting on her shoulder. "First things first. Let's go rescue Dillon's mom."

"Yeah, for all we know, those squirrels may have taken her prisoner," said Mikey.

"We'll check the Fresh Mart first," said Dillon. "Let's go!"

⦿ ⦿ ⦿

 53

Dillon's mom's station wagon was indeed in the parking lot of Fresh Mart. A lot of cars were. According to a big sign out front, hamburgers and hot dogs were half price, and watermelons were buy one, get one free. It was summer, and weekend watermelon and cookouts were going to happen, heat or no heat.

But it wasn't the sign or the watermelon that caught their attention (although watermelon sounded very refreshing right now, considering they'd been running from one end of Main Street to the other under the suffocating summer sun); it was the wall of shopping carts that had been dragged in front of the Fresh Mart doors. And on the other side of that shopping cart barrier, behind the closed glass doors, a group of people pressed their hands and faces against the glass. They were saying something, but no one could hear them.

"They're trying to tell us something," said Mikey. "But I have no idea what."

"Be kind to stew," said Samantha von Oppelstein. She smiled and then added, "I can read lips."

"That makes zero sense," said Madeline.

"Yeah," said Dillon. "Is Stew a person? Or like beef stew?"

Mikey elbowed Dillon and pointed his foam finger at the front window. "Look, it's your mom!"

Sure enough, there was Dillon's mom. She lifted a piece of cardboard up and pressed it against the glass.

Behind you!

All four kids slowly turned around. A line of squirrels, at least thirty long and five squirrels deep, waited across the street, just on this side of the bridge (the metal one on South Main, where the troll lived—the troll who'd steal your toes if you didn't spit over the side). Their angry eyes fixed on Dillon. Their tails twitched ever so slightly. Their little claws clicked together.

"Look at the creek," whispered Samantha von Oppelstein. "They've cut off this end of town too."

"They must have blocked it downstream, by the lake," said Madeline.

Wolf Creek had risen to the top of the bank and was already beginning to spill over the sides of the South Main bridge. If this bridge was flooded out, then the bridge out of town—the one on Cemetery Road, near Lake Pond—would be out too.

The trap was closing in. Escape from Wolver Hollow seemed impossible.

More squirrels appeared atop Fresh Mart, a line of squirrels all the way across the building. The sun was behind them, casting long, dark, menacing squirrel shadows on the parking lot.

"Now what?" Mikey asked.

Dillon thought about what Madeline had said, about being tactically smart. The squirrels might have closed off the roads, but they hadn't thought to close down communication. If Dillon could alert the whole town, let everyone know what was going on,

 57

the people of Wolver Hollow could work together to defend against the squirrel threat.

"We have to go to the radio station," Dillon said. "We have to get the word out to everyone."

"We can send an emergency warning," said Madeline. "The kind that blares out across town and interrupts the regular programming."

The big squirrel with the white chin fur emerged from behind the line of roof squirrels. It raised one paw in the air. Every squirrel tail stopped twitching. When it brought its paw down, in one swift motion, the horde of squirrels by the bridge dropped to all fours and scurried toward the kids.

"Run!" screamed Mikey.

7

There's nothing like a horde of fast, angry squirrels to make you run for dear life. And run for dear life they did, indeed. But remember, they had already run all the way to the Fresh Mart from the north end of Main Street, and now they were going to have to run all the way back, since the WOLF radio station, the voice of Wolver Hollow, was back where they'd started.

They ran, turning every so often to swat a squirrel or two away with a broom, or foam finger, or block a diving squirrel attack with a Frisbee. They raced past the bronze statue of François Gildebrand Soufflé, the town's founder, and past town hall, but the squirrels were quickly gaining on them. Soon, they'd be overrun by the sheer number of angry, chittering, furry beasts. No amount of foam finger swatting or broom swinging would save them.

The streets were eerily quiet, not a person in sight or a car moving. It was like a ghost town.

"We're not going to make it," said Dillon.

Two quick whoop-whoops of a police siren sounded, and Sheriff Macklin's patrol car pulled up behind them, sending squirrels scampering in all directions so they didn't get run over.

The squirrels darted to both sides of the street, taking to the narrow alleys between buildings and the shadows, waiting for the right moment to strike.

Officer Macklin rolled down his window and lifted a megaphone to his lips. His mirrored sunglasses were fixed on them. He didn't seem to notice the squirrels at all.

"This is Sheriff Macklin," he said.

"We know who you are," Dillon muttered.

"I'm going to need you to go to your homes immediately," said the sheriff. "Wolver Hollow is under a state of emergency."

"The squirrels?" Dillon asked.

"Squirrels?" he repeated.

 61

"The squirrels are attacking," said Mikey.
"They're everywhere. They're after Dillon."

Sheriff Macklin just looked at them through
his mirrored sunglasses for a good ten seconds.

"Squirrels," he said.

"In groups," added Madeline.

"They were just chasing us," said Samantha von Oppelstein.

"So you're telling me that the squirrels are responsible for the north road being blocked?'

"Yes," said the kids.

"And flooding the river?"

"Yes," they all said, in unison.

A bright flash and an arc of electricity crackled from across town, where the power plant was. The marquee lights of the playhouse, which were lit even during the day, went dark.

"And the power going out?" asked Sheriff Macklin. "That was all 'squirrels'?"

He made little air quotes when he said "squirrels," as if they didn't exist.

"You have to believe us," said Dillon. "Look, there's a bunch right over there!"

But when they all looked to where Dillon pointed, there were no squirrels to be seen.

"Where'd they go?" whispered Madeline.

"You've got to get up pretty early to pull one over on ol' Sheriff Macklin," said the sheriff. "Squirrels . . ." He chuckled and then spoke back into his microphone. "All right, kids, town emergency response Bravo 4-7 in effect. Go straight home and stay off the roads . . . and the bridges . . . and don't go near the river . . . pretty much just stay in your rooms."

"Yes, Sheriff Macklin," they all said.

He nodded, rolled up his window, and drove off with two quick whoop-whoops of his siren.

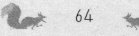

"Now what?" Mikey asked.

"The radio station idea is out of the question," said Madeline. "No power means no broadcasting."

"We can't just go home," said Dillon.

Red eyes started to gather in the shadows again. The squirrels were gathering.

"We need answers," said Samantha von Oppelstein. She turned and pointed at the columned building across the street. "We need to go to . . . the library."

8

Dillon, Mikey, Madeline, and Samantha
von Oppelstein hurried across the street to the
library. Dillon opened the rusted metal gate
and took the old, steep steps two at a time.
They had just reached the top step, and the
two marble pillars, when the squirrels scampered over and through the metal fence.

"Hurry," said Mikey.

Dillon pulled the doors open and all four

kids practically fell over one another in their desperation to get inside before the squirrels got to them. Those long, sharp teeth and claws were terrifying.

Samantha von Oppelstein slammed the doors closed behind them.

With the power out, the library was even more creepy than it normally was. Sunlight filtered through the few tall, narrow windows, casting long shadows across the chairs, tables, and shelves of the first floor. A broad set of stairs curved up to the second-floor balcony, where taller shelves stretched deeper into the recesses of the library. Old men and women from Wolver Hollow's history stared down at them from their framed paintings on the wall.

It was quiet. So quiet that the scratching of

the squirrels on the front door seemed to echo through the still library.

"Hello?" Dillon called out. "Anybody here?"

His words hung in the air like the dust particles drifting in the rays of sunlight.

Dillon cupped his hands together and called out. "Anyone? Someone? Miss Librarian lady? We're um . . . we're looking for—"

"*Sciurus carolinensis,*" said a voice from behind them. "The eastern gray squirrel."

Dillon and Mikey jumped toward each other, got tangled up, and fell down. Madeline slapped her hands to her mouth to stifle her shriek, and Samantha von Oppelstein waved.

"Hi, Ms. Yaga," said Samantha von Oppelstein.

"Hello dear," said the Librarian (Ms. Yaga).

"She has a name," Dillon whispered to Mikey.

Neither of them spent much time in the library, but they (like most kids in Wolver Hollow) had never known the Librarian to be known as anything but "the Librarian."

"I help shelve books after school," said Samantha von Oppelstein, shrugging.

"And I don't know what I'd do without you, dear," said the Librarian. "I do wish they'd stop scratching at my doors."

Dillon, Mikey, Madeline, and Samantha von Oppelstein looked toward the doors, afraid they'd find the squirrels scratching their way through. But that was impossible, they thought. The doors were metal, not wood.

"Ah, here we go," said the Librarian,

69

suddenly behind the checkout counter, across the room. She dropped a heavy book on the counter with a thumping thud.

Dillon's and Mikey's eyes widened.

"How did—"

"But she—"

Samantha von Oppelstein raised her eyebrows and smiled. Madeline scratched her head. They'd only turned around for half a second.

"Well," said the Librarian, "are you all going to stand over there all day, gawking, or are you going to come get the answers you seek?"

All four kids rushed to the long, curved counter.

The Librarian flipped a few old pages, dragging a yellowed fingernail along the old, typewritten text. A picture of a gray squirrel stood out from the dense passage.

"Yes, here we go," said the Librarian. She pulled her glasses down to the edge of her nose and practically pressed her face into the book. "Oh, that's interesting. . . ."

"What?" asked Dillon. "What's interesting?"

The Librarian jabbed her fingernail at one paragraph. "The gray squirrel normally lives alone, and not in groups. But sometimes, especially in severe cold spells, they form groups, called 'scurries.'"

Dillon scrunched his eyebrows. None of this made sense. It was summer, it was hot . . . why would all these squirrels form a scurry now?

"Good question," said the Librarian. "They must be preparing, storing food early. Looks like we're going to be in for a *very, very* cold winter."

Dillon's jaw dropped. "Did you just read my mind?"

The Librarian grinned and leaned forward over the book.

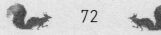

"You took something from them," she said.

Dillon nodded. "Sour Sugar Snakes."

"They also form their own chain of command," she said. "The toughest is the boss."

"That's silly," said Madeline. "It should be the smartest."

"Or the spookiest," said Samantha von Oppelstein. She tugged at her bat earrings.

"The squirrel with the white patch on its chin," said Dillon. "That must be the leader."

"The one you knocked out of the tree?" Mikey asked.

The Librarian frowned.

"It was an accident," said Dillon. "I just meant to scare it into dropping my Sour Sugar Snakes!"

"Well, you have to make things right with

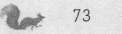 73

that squirrel," said the Librarian. "Find that squirrel and offer it your Sour Sugar Snakes, and perhaps you'll be done with this whole business."

"But we haven't seen that squirrel since the Fresh Mart," said Dillon.

"Follow the squirrels, and they will take you to him," said the Librarian. She turned the book toward them and pointed to another passage.

All four kids leaned over to read the text.

"Red foxes are their biggest predator," said Samantha von Oppelstein. "If we get foxes to come chase the squirrels, the squirrels will run to their nest."

"And that's probably where the king of the squirrels lives," said Mikey.

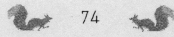

"Could be a queen, you know," said Samantha von Oppelstein.

"But how do we lure foxes?" Dillon asked.

When he looked up, the Librarian was no longer standing there. A small bowl of berries sat on the counter.

"Where'd she go?" Dillon asked. "She was *just* standing here."

"Blackberries!" said Madeline. "I remember my grandmother talking about keeping the foxes away from her chickens by planting blackberry bushes!"

"And the woods are filled with blackberries," said Mikey. He was a Wolf Scout, and he knew just where to find ripe blackberries.

"And foxes," said Madeline.

"And ghosts," said Samantha von Oppelstein.

The other kids just stared at her.

"Well, maybe," said Samantha von Oppelstein. "We can't rule anything out."

Dillon looked around the library. There was no sign of the Librarian anywhere.

"Yeah," he said, "can't rule anything out. Okay, we'll split into two groups. Samantha von Oppelstein and Madeline, your mission, if you choose to accept it, is to go to the comic shop and get as many bags of Sour Sugar Snakes as you can."

Samantha von Oppelstein saluted and Madeline said, "Aye, aye."

"Mikey and I will go into the woods and gather blackberries," Dillon continued. He totally felt like Captain Duke Ross right now. "We'll leave a trail for the foxes. Let's all meet at the gazebo. Operation Red Fox is now a go."

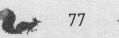

9

Dillon and Mikey snuck out the front
doors first. The squirrels must have gotten tired
of scratching at the steel doors, and had either
gone off to cause more mischief and mayhem,
or were looking for another way in. Or maybe,
maybe they were waiting to ambush the kids.
That idea made Dillon shiver.

They hid behind the columns first, to be
sure, but no squirrels attacked.

"It's too quiet," said Mikey. "I don't like it."

"Listen," said Dillon.

A few car alarms blared from back in the direction of Pine Street and Hill Crest. Dogs barked, and cats hissed and spat and made the kinds of loud noises cats make when they fight. Sheriff Macklin's patrol car whoop-whooped down the street.

"The squirrels must be back near our houses, waiting for me to come home," said Dillon. "That's where all that noise is coming from."

"Then we should be able to make it to the woods without too much trouble," said Mikey. "Let's stick to the tree line along the cemetery fence and stay out of sight."

They looked back over their shoulders and gave the girls a thumbs-up.

 79

"Good luck," Madeline whispered.

"We'll meet you at the gazebo," said Samantha von Oppelstein.

The boys nodded and then rushed down the steps and around the ivy-covered corner of the library.

The old cemetery ran the entire length of North Main Street, separated from the backs of businesses by a thin stretch of pine trees. It was enough to give the boys cover and keep them away from prying squirrel eyes. By the time they reached the church, they could see the old windmill. The woods they wanted, the area where Mikey said they could find the best blackberries, was right across from that.

Every scraping branch made them jump.

 80

Every broken twig made them freeze. They imagined that even now, the squirrels could be watching them, ready to leap down onto their heads or run back to "Patch" (that was what they had decided to call the leader—king or queen—of the squirrels).

They had just reached the last section of the cemetery fence, the area where the rickety old windmill looked over the north end of town, when the first bloodcurdling squirrel screams almost burst their eardrums.

Squirrels leapt from branches and ran at them, on all fours—long, curved front teeth bared to bite.

Mikey swatted one away with his foam hand and jabbed another squirrel back with the soft index finger. Dillon ducked an

 81

incoming squirrel and pelted another with one of his tennis balls.

"Go, go, go!" said Dillon.

A squirrel clung to the back of his shirt, but Mikey batted it off.

The boys sprinted across North Main, directly on the other side of the fallen tree roadblock. Dillon spun around and whipped a tennis ball at a squirrel that was closing in on him.

"One left!" he shouted to Mikey, holding up his last tennis ball.

Mikey pointed his foam finger forward. "We're almost there!"

The woods here were thick and dark and mysterious. These were cold woods, the kind of forest where even the sun was afraid to

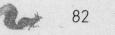

shine. One road cut through it, leading to the Torrance Hotel, a popular winter destination for skiers and for fall hikers who wanted to watch the leaves change. But in the summer, it was pretty quiet. The only other landmark out this way was the long, lonely road to Canada and Dewart Hospital (a place with its own secrets and dangers). But Dillon and Mikey were not near any of those things. They plunged into the shroud of deep, dense, inky stillness.

They ran until the road was no longer in sight. The sun wasn't visible above the canopy. There was nothing but trees and roots and rocks and an unsettling stillness.

"No squirrels," said Dillon. "Why are there no squirrels?"

 83

"I don't know," said Mikey. "Maybe this place is too creepy, even for them."

"What was that?" Dillon asked.

"What was what?"

"I don't know. I thought I heard something."

Dillon and Mikey stood back-to-back, watching for any signs of attack squirrels, or anything else that might decide it wanted to taste the blood and bones of two fifth graders. Everyone knew that terrible things lurked deeper in these woods, things like windigos and witches and wolves the size of cows.

"How far until we find the blackberries?" Dillon whispered.

"Not far," Mikey whispered back.

They moved cautiously through the forest, back-to-back or shoulder to shoulder, watch-

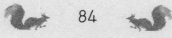

84

ing for anything that might want to hurt them. Mikey remembered what to look for, the way the rocks and roots grew and which bushes and fungal patches had marked their trail when his Wolf Scout pack had come out for an afternoon of wild foraging.

"There," said Mikey. "Right up there, in that clearing."

Dillon followed Mikey's foam finger. There was a small grove ahead where the trees thinned out enough to let a decent-sized patch of light in, and from the look of things, it was surrounded by wild, bountiful blackberry bushes.

Dillon followed Mikey forward, creeping toward the clearing.

"Look at them all," said Dillon.

"Told you," said Mikey.

"We'll fill the fronts of our shirts with as many blackberries as we can carry," said Dillon.

"Let's hurry," said Mikey. "This place really freaks me out."

Behind them, a set of golden eyes glowed in the underbrush. It was joined by another, and then another, and then six more. All watching. All staring.

10

Dillon and Mikey picked as many blackberries as their shirts could hold. They stretched the bottoms of their shirts out before them, so that the T-shirts became kind of like baskets. They packed in so many berries that even one more would just spill out. Their fingers were stained a deep blue, almost black, and they had several cuts and scratches from thorns.

The bushes rustled behind them. Dillon and Mikey froze and then, ever so slowly, turned to see what had caused the noise. A pack of foxes sat watching them, their golden eyes fixed on the berries piled in the boys' shirts. The largest fox licked its front teeth. Several of the foxes uttered a low growl.

Mikey dropped a couple of blackberries in front of him and took a few steps backward.

"Move slowly," he said to Dillon. "Nice and easy. They just want the berries, and if they don't have to fight for them, they won't."

Dillon followed Mikey's lead. "You learned this in Wolf Scouts?"

"Yep."

Dillon dropped a few blackberries. "If we

 88

somehow survive this, if there's still a town standing after the squirrels are done with it, I'm joining Wolf Scouts."

They walked steadily backward, taking turns dropping berries. The foxes loped after them, eating up the blackberries. They kept their eyes peeled for any signs of squirrels, especially above them, on the branches and in the trees. They could be anywhere, waiting to attack.

As they neared the road, several squirrels waited for them on low-hanging branches. But when the squirrels saw the foxes, they emitted a high-pitched warning scream, then ran off, jumping from branch to branch, and then across the power lines and up and over rooftops.

"It's working!" said Dillon. "They're scared of the foxes!"

"And there they go!" said Mikey.

When the foxes saw the squirrels, they forgot all about the blackberries. They charged after them, out of the woods and down the street, following the path of the escaping squirrels.

Dillon and Mikey dropped the rest of their blackberries and chased after the foxes, but the foxes were too quick and were soon lost to sight. The squirrels had hopped and leapt and scampered back toward the center of town, and the foxes had followed.

"I wonder how Madeline and Samantha von Oppelstein did?" Dillon asked. He had to slow down to catch his breath.

 91

"Hey, do you get the feeling we're being watched?" Mikey asked.

He and Dillon walked down the center of North Main Street, turning every so often to see if they were being followed or watched. Every store was closed, every curtain drawn, every window shut, despite the summer heat.

"This is so eerie," said Dillon.

A sign hung in the window of Pizza Mario's:

CLOSED DUE TO SQUIRRELS

SEND HELP!

Sheriff Macklin's police car was parked halfway on the sidewalk in front of town hall. The driver's-side door was open, and the light was still spinning, throwing red and blue lights against the building. But there was no sign of the sheriff. His radio crackled on and off.

"*. . . reports of squirrels tearing up flower beds . . .*"

"*. . . Pine Street, we have a report of squirrels pouring acorns down a chimney . . .*"

"*. . . squirrels marching toward . . .*"

"*. . . squirrels on the roof . . .*"

"*. . . squirrels . . . squirrels . . . squirrels . . .*"

"We're too late," said Dillon. "The squirrels have taken over the town!"

"But what about the foxes?" Mikey asked. "The foxes should have chased them all out!"

Dillon stopped in his tracks and grabbed Mikey's sleeve.

"Look," Dillon said. "The foxes."

The gazebo where Dillon and Mikey were supposed to meet Madeline and Samantha von Oppelstein was surrounded by overturned shopping carts. Foxes had been trapped under each one, stuck in shopping-cart cages.

There were three other upright carts, with a second cart flipped upside down and stacked on top to make a rolling cage. Those weren't filled with foxes. One of them contained Madeline and Samantha von Oppelstein.

Squirrels perched atop the gazebo and surrounded the cart cages. They filled the little park and appeared on top of the mayor's office and the library. They sat on the bronze

head and shoulders of the statue of François Gildebrand Soufflé.

Squirrels hopped and scampered out from hidden places to line the street behind them, cutting off any chance of an escape.

They'd walked right into a trap.

 96

11

"Where's their leader?" Dillon asked. "I don't see Patch anywhere."

"There's so many of them," said Mikey. "Could be anywhere, hiding among them."

The line of squirrels behind them moved forward, chattering and squealing and nipping at their heels.

"Ow, okay, we're going!" said Dillon.

It was obvious that the squirrels wanted the

boys to go to the squirrels in the park. There was no choice but to do what the squirrels wanted. They were outnumbered and surrounded on all sides.

When the boys got closer, they saw that Madeline and Samantha von Oppelstein were unhurt. Scared, and trapped, but not hurt.

"Are you okay?" Dillon whispered.

"For now," said Madeline. "But what are they going to do with us?"

"They'll probably make a big acorn soup and put us in it," said Samantha von Oppelstein. "Or maybe they'll bury us in a hole like they bury their acorns. I'll bet that's it. That's what they'll probably do."

"Why would you say that?" Mikey asked, suddenly even more terrified than he already

 98

was. "You might be giving them ideas."

Two squirrels tugged at Mikey's shoelaces and pointed toward the empty shopping-cart cage. Another squirrel tugged the foam hand free from Mikey's own hand. It ran to the gazebo and dropped it in the pile with Madeline's Frisbee and Samantha von Oppelstein's broom. The foxes shifted back and forth in their own cells, whining and scratching at the grass. Anytime a fox tried to bite at its cage, or dig under it, five or six squirrels pelted it with acorns. The foxes very quickly gave up trying to dig their way out and sat staring, teeth bared. Mikey climbed into the cage, and the squirrels set another shopping cart on top, trapping him inside.

 99

"You've got to do something, Dillon," said Mikey. "Get us out of here."

"My foot's asleep," said Madeline. "It's cramped in here."

"I'm thinking," said Dillon. "Did you get the candy?"

Samantha von Oppelstein shook her head no. "They captured us before we could get there."

SQUEAK SQUEAK CHATTER CHATTER SQUEAK!

One squirrel leapt onto Dillon's shoulder and wrapped its tail around his mouth. Another pulled his last tennis ball from his hand and held it over its head, triumphantly waving it in the air.

Every squirrel, from the park, to the street,

to the rooftops, shook their tails and let out ear-piercing squeals. They had captured the enemy and taken the weapon that had started this war in the first place: the tennis ball.

Dillon held his hands in the air. "I surrender!"

 101

A squirrel with the tennis ball hopped before him, jabbing a claw in the air and chattering angrily.

SQUEAK SQUEAK SQUEAK SQUEAK SQUEAK!

"I didn't mean it," he said. "It was an accident! Just . . . just don't hurt my friends, okay?"

The squirrel shook the tennis ball at Dillon and then pointed past the gazebo, past the statue of François Gildebrand Soufflé, in the direction of Cemetery Road. The crowd of squirrels parted for him to pass. They wanted him to walk, and as soon as he took a few steps in the right direction, squirrels closed in behind him, forcing him forward.

They watched him as he passed, shaking their tails and sniffing the air. Some clicked their teeth or claws together. Others shoved acorns into their cheeks, ready to pelt him should he make any sudden moves.

Dillon knew where they were taking him. They had to be taking him to see the leader, to see Patch. And from the look of things, they were taking him out of town, out past the Gas-n-Go, out toward the Witching Tree.

Nothing good ever happened at the Witching Tree.

Legends said that shortly after the town was founded, a man was bitten by a wolf under the full moon, and one month later, he returned as half man, half wolf—a wolfman. Several other early settlers were attacked by the wolfman, and every one of them turned into a werewolf one month later. No one ever

did find out what happened to them, and if you listened closely, during a full moon, you could hear them out by the Witching Tree, howling.

Some legends spoke of the Wailing Woman, a ghostly bride whose new husband went out to chop the Witching Tree down for firewood and never came back. All that was found was his bloody axe. The Wailing Woman haunts the tree where he was last seen.

And then, of course, the very story that gave the tree its name in the first place—the witches of Wolver Hollow, a secret coven of witches who ate little children and cursed those who crossed them. The Witching Tree was their meeting place, and witches gathered for secret meetings to practice dark rituals and even darker magic.

And now Dillon was being guided to that very tree.

He shivered, despite the summer heat.

Nothing good ever happened at the Witching Tree.

12

The Witching Tree was tall and gnarly and bent and twisted in odd ways. It never grew leaves, not even a single bud in spring, and was blackened on one side, where it had been struck by lightning three times since the founding of Wolver Hollow.

No one went near it, not even the adults who waved their hands and said all those old stories were folktales, spooky stories made up to keep kids from getting into trouble out there on the edge of town. But you never caught a single adult, not one, ever going out to the Witching Tree. And no one was ever brave enough to try cutting it down, not after what happened to the Wailing Woman's husband.

And now Dillon was headed straight for that tree, pushed along by a horde of angry, vengeful squirrels. He was glad it was still daylight. He couldn't imagine coming out here at night, no way.

The old tree sat right on the bend of Cemetery Road, towering and twisted and menacing. Part of its branches stretched over the cemetery wall, skeletal twigs waving at the rows and rows of cracked and weathered tombstones. But the branches on this side

 107

of the cemetery, the branches that seemed to reach for him like withered claws, like witches' claws, were now filled with squirrels. Patch stood on the top branch, alone on the limb. His white chin fur was visible from the bottom of the tree.

Squirrels fanned out around the tree and behind Dillon. The squirrel with Dillon's tennis ball dashed up the side of the tree, clawing its way up the trunk and leaping from branch to branch. It presented the tennis ball to Patch.

Patch clamped one clawed foot down on the tennis ball, holding it on the branch with its furry toes.

"*SQUEAK SQUEAK SQUEAK-SQUEAK SQUEAKITY SQUEAK,*" Patch said.

 109

Somehow, Dillon understood what Patch was saying. Somehow, he could understand Squirrel. There was no doubt about it, thought Dillon; it had to be the magic of the Witching Tree.

"Fellow squirrels," said Patch, "before you stands the two-legged attacker of our kind. The stealer of our food, the—"

"I didn't steal anything!" Dillon blurted out, without thinking. "You took that candy from *my* tree house!"

"*I* found it!" said Patch.

"In *my* tree house!"

Patch scratched his chin and held up the tennis ball.

"And then you dared to strike me with your fuzzy green ball of death!"

The squirrels all shook their tails and clicked their teeth.

"It was an accident!" said Dillon. "I wasn't *trying* to hit you."

"So you admit to throwing it?" Patch asked.

The squirrels all watched and waited for Dillon's answer. Patch waited for Dillon's answer.

Dillon thought about his friends in shopping-cart cages and all the people of Wolver Hollow who had barricaded themselves inside their homes and businesses. He had started this whole mess, accident or not, and it was up to him to get them all out of it.

He thought back to what Ms. Yaga, the Librarian, had said: *The toughest is the boss,* and something about squirrels forming scurries when bad winters were coming.

Dillon thought about Captain Duke Ross of the Mars Expeditionary Force. He'd been in situations just like this: outnumbered, facing certain defeat, but somehow he always triumphed. Somehow he always managed to find some courage.

He shoved his hands into his pockets and felt something in his right pocket. Something crinkly, something plastic. Of course! The last pack of Sour Sugar Snakes.

"Squirrels," Dillon said, looking around at the mass of gray-furred creatures. "Isn't the strongest of you supposed to be the leader?"

The squirrels chattered and squealed

112

among themselves. One gray-white, wizened squirrel, at the foot of the tree, spoke up. "It is, yes. You know our law?"

"Only some," said Dillon. "But I know that the strongest cannot be a squirrel knocked out of a tree by one tennis ball."

The squirrels all started chittering and squeaking again.

"Do not listen to this two-legs!" said Patch. "He is trying to trick us! Any one of you would have been knocked down by his weapon!"

"He's right," said Dillon. "And I'm not trying to say that he should not be your leader! I just want you to listen to me for a minute. I have an offer to make."

The squirrels all looked to the older

 113

squirrel. The older squirrel looked up to Patch and nodded.

Patch nodded back. It had been confirmed: he was still in charge.

"Speak your words, young two-legs," said Patch.

"I know that a bad winter is coming," said Dillon. "That's the only reason you're all gathered together, right? In one big group? Well, I can help you."

"Help us how?" Patch asked.

"I can bring you extra food this winter," Dillon said. "Bread and nuts and vegetables and snacks. Even . . ."

Dillon reached into his pocket and drew out the pack of Sour Sugar Snakes.

". . . even sweet treats like the kind you

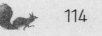

found in my tree house," said Dillon. "I'll leave a supply of food for you each week, outside my tree house." He held the pack of Sour Sugar Snakes up. "Starting with these. These are for you."

Patch tossed the tennis ball to another squirrel and leapt three branches down, sniffing the air. "And what do you want, hmmm?"

Dillon tossed the candy up to Patch.

"Call it even? Let my friends go and stop invading the town?"

Patch pounced back up to his top branch, Sour Sugar Snakes in his mouth.

Dillon watched him. The squirrels watched him.

Patch ripped the corner off the plastic and stuffed a Sour Sugar Snake into his mouth.

 115

He chewed it up and said, "You have a deal, young two-legs. And . . ."

"And?" Dillon asked.

Patch scampered down a few branches and snatched the tennis ball from the other squirrel. He tossed it down to Dillon.

"No more 'accidents,'" Patch said.

Dillon nodded and shoved the tennis ball into his pocket. "Deal."

13

Two weeks later, Dillon Ford sat in his bedroom, reading the latest Captain Duke Ross comic book. His friends had been freed, the townsfolk and foxes had been released, the roads and bridges had been cleared, the power was back on, and the squirrels had gone back to doing what squirrels do.

The *Wolver Hollow Gazette* called the whole thing a "series of unnatural coincidences":

The summer heat had caused the trees to be uprooted and to block the roads and dam the river, which had caused the squirrels to flood into the town, and those squirrels had accidentally cut the power. That was the truth everyone believed.

Everyone but Dillon, Mikey, Madeline, and Samantha von Oppelstein.

Where everyone else saw squirrels running along fences, scurrying up trees, stealing from bird feeders, and hopping through the grass, Dillon and his friends saw an army that they had a temporary alliance with.

As long as they left the squirrels food each week, all was well.

They left fruit, nuts, lettuce, seeds, bread, and, of course, Sour Sugar Snakes outside

 118

Dillon's tree house each week. And each week, Patch and a group of squirrels came to collect to store for the coming winter.

Week after week after week. Until the last week of summer.

When Dillon climbed up into his tree house to read some comics and drink lemonade, he found all the food they'd left for the squirrels that week still sitting there. It hadn't been collected. Not one piece of it.

The squirrels had never missed a collection.

He climbed back down out of the tree house, scratching his head. And that was when he saw it, a single word scratched into the tree, right next to the ladder:

SQUEAK

Dillon traced his fingers along each letter.

He had no idea what it meant, or where the squirrels had gone, or if they'd ever be back.

Because to this day, no squirrels have been seen in Wolver Hollow since the end of that crazy summer.

But . . . deep in the woods, in the shadows of the pines and tangled bushes, another group of critters gathered. A group not too happy about being lured out of their dens by blackberries. Not happy about being caged by squirrels. And certainly not happy about being left out of Dillon's deal.

This group, with golden eyes and red fur, plotted and planned.

But that is another story.

And
that, my
friends, is what
happened that fateful
summer. It started with one
thrown tennis ball and almost ended
with the demise of Wolver Hollow.
Where *did* the squirrels go? What
did that single *SQUEAK*, carved into
the tree, mean? Was it a warning?
A threat? We may never know. . . .
But I have heard it said that many
towns, cities, and neighborhoods
like your own have more and more
squirrels in them. Squirrels plotting

and
planning
and
whispering
clever schemes.
If you see two
squirrels together, you can be
sure that they're up to something
clever, some bit of mischief. And if
I were you, I'd leave them a little
treat, just to get on their good side.
Remember, they have strength in
numbers. And very, very sharp teeth.

Acknowledgments

I'd like to thank the squirrels at Trap Pond State Park in Delaware for raiding the kids' tents, scampering around our campsite, and otherwise being general nuisances. Yes, I hit one of you with a football, but it was a toss. And honestly, I never thought I'd come close to hitting you. You jumped up and ran off, but look—because of that moment, we have a story! And hey, karma, right? A day or two later I wound up in the ER from a volleyball-related injury. So we're even? Although, really, I think you come out on top. You get a whole book, and I got an ER visit and a hospital bill.

Water under the bridge. Unless you mean the bridge on South Main Street—there's a troll under that bridge.

And while we're talking of Trap Pond, I'd like to thank our kids, from oldest to youngest: Zachary, Ainsley, Shane, Logan, Braeden, and Sawyer. You broiled in your tents and suffered without WiFi. (The horror of it all!) And yes, Charlotte's scrunchie is *not* Shane's stinky socks, but . . . who knew? So thank you, and . . . look before you throw things in the fire.

As always, I owe a tremendous amount of thanks to my amazing agent, Jennifer Soloway. I am so proud to have you in my corner and count myself as one lucky author to have you representing me. We have so much more to do!

Karen Nagel . . . I have grown so much as a writer working with you. Can you believe we've done (will do, are in the midst of doing?) twelve books together so far?! I've learned a lot from you, and I look forward to learning more. Thank you!

Thank you, Teo, for being so amazing. We've been having a lot of fun building this world, and Teo keeps dropping in fun little Easter eggs and little surprises. And we're both waiting for the Night Frights theme park!

I'm going to keep this shorter than my normal habit of long-winded acknowledgments. What's that? It's about time I figured that out? Lol . . . What can I say? These things are fun!

So I'll end this with a great big, super huge

 127

thank-you to the love of my life, my adventure partner, writing companion, best friend, amazing wife, and tremendous inspiration, Jessica Rinker. Thank you for being by my side. Put simply: you rock, shield-maiden. Skol!

Looking for another great book?
Find it
IN THE MIDDLE.

Fun, fantastic books for kids
in the in-be**TWEEN** age.

IntheMiddleBooks.com

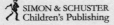